Ropes of doubt

(still waiting for her)

<u>Written by</u>

Alaa Zaher

The material and intellectual ownership of this book is subject only to the author, and any modification or copying of the contents of this book without the author's approval will be considered an infringement of the author's intellectual and material rights, as well as the personalities within the book from the author's inspiration, and has no connection to reality and if it is found in reality it is a coincidence. This is a work of fiction. Similarities to real people, places, or events are entirely coincidental.

Copyright © 2024 Alaa Zaher.

Written by Alaa Zaher.

Chapter One

Ink tears flowed from my fingers, the words call out to you, but there is no way to reach you. I write to you as I embrace the loss, I write to you with nothing between us but this paper, pouring out the pain of the slow-moving days.

I find nothing but your shadow moving ahead of me, a distant light that I cannot reach. I touch the emptiness in the air, as if you are there, just a step away, but I cannot reach you. I write to you, and between every letter and letter, a burning question resides in me: When will fate grant us a meeting? Despite this emptiness, I cannot stop waiting for you. Because I know, deep in my heart, that the road leading to you might be longer than I imagine, but in the end, it will take me to you.

I might continue to grasp at emptiness, chase the mirage, but this is the destiny written for both you and me, to be part of this longing. I live in two parallel worlds... one where you are, and the other is nothing but you. You are there, in a distant place, and I am here, but we are together in every heartbeat, in every thought, in every dream that travels me to you. Your absence does not mean separation, and even if you are far away, your presence in my heart is stronger than any distance.

But, as the days pass, I begin to sense in the silence of the night that absence is stealing a part of my soul, and the further you are, the heavier the burden of waiting on my heart. I search for you in every face, in every corner, in every moment I live, as if the whole world has become empty except for you. But, every time I reach out to you through the emptiness, I discover that your heart is still far away.

It is no longer enough to hear your voice in a dream, nor to see your face in memories, the space between us has become colder, and the times lonelier. Although our love was once stronger than any distance, each time, it makes me question: Can love alone be enough to overcome these distances, or will the memories continue to haunt me forever?

Will you return to me one day, or will our meeting remain an endless dream? I will remain here, on the edge of waiting, anticipating every moment that might carry me to you, even though the distances have worn me out, my heart continues to expand for you, and keeps beating for you despite everything. Every time I close my eyes, I return to those moments we shared together, as if they were everything in this world, but when I open my eyes, I find myself returning to reality, where you are far away, and I am here, alone in my waiting.

I find myself returning to that crucial moment between dream and reality, between a past lived with love and warmth, and a present enveloped in silence and waiting. I return repeatedly, even though I know I will return alone, surrounded by remnants of memories and the echo of words that are no longer spoken.

In this empty world, where places become a haven for your images, I move through your details and search in the emptiness for remnants of your specter.

I know that I am walking on an endless path, a path drawn by distances, with chains tightening around me, but I have no choice but to keep walking. Each step I take weighs me down even more, as if this eternal wait has infiltrated my soul, making every heartbeat an expression of a love that refuses to extinguish, and a sorrow that deepens.

I have told myself time and time again that I must forget, but how can I escape myself? This is my story, the tale of a man who chose to remain on the edge of meeting, waiting for a moment that may never come, or maybe it will...

But he knows that his heart no longer understands any language but longing, and will never know any path other than the road to **you**.

Maybe it was a coincidence, or maybe it was a destiny written before we were born, but in that moment, I felt something I did not understand and did not dare to ignore. The sky was slowly darkening, as if the night was quietly creeping in to embrace the city, when that light storm of rain began.

I had left the café next to the library late as usual, trying to escape the pressures of work and the empty conversations of people. As I ran across the wet sidewalk, a small sign stopped me, written on it: "Clearance Sale of Old Books".

I had never thought of entering before, but suddenly nostalgia overwhelmed me... I entered the old library, and the first thing that caught my attention was the smell; the aroma of old paper and the whispers of books closed on their secrets. The place was almost deserted, with only an old seller sitting in a distant corner, staring at a book, as if everyone around him did not exist.

I approached the rickety shelves, looking for a specific book that reminded me of my childhood days, not knowing that I would find more than that. I noticed a girl standing alone in a distant corner, holding a book in her hands, as if she did not want anyone to notice her presence.

I could not see her features clearly, but something about her was drawing me, making me watch her from afar without realizing why.

She was **Lucy**, as I later found out, but at that time, she was just a stranger with something vague in her face, a beauty that did not declare itself easily. At first, I ignored her, but there was something in her isolation that attracted me, as if she were immersed in her book and everything around her did not matter.

I slowly approached the bookshelf next to her, hoping to find a book that would distract me from my strange desire to know who she was. I did not expect her to initiate the conversation, but she, without lifting her eyes from the book, said in a calm tone, carrying an unusual coldness:

"It is not polite to watch strangers. Do you think you are the only one seeking quiet here?"

I froze in place for a moment, surprised by her directness, and awkwardly did not have a suitable response.

I smiled lightly, trying to ease the tension of the moment, but she remained steadfast in her gaze, showing no interest in my spontaneous smile. It was as if she had placed an invisible barrier between us, a barrier that felt stronger than any desire to start a conversation with her.

I stammered a bit, trying to justify my gaze: "I apologize... I didn't mean... I was just..."

She interrupted me, in a cold tone, without looking at me: "I didn't mean to start a conversation. Please, I just want peace."

Her response was harsh, but it only piqued my curiosity more. I couldn't understand why I felt an overwhelming urge to talk to her, a desire not just out of curiosity, but as if something was drawing me towards her despite the obvious barrier she was trying to set.

I stood there for a few moments, torn between the desire to talk to her and the fear of disturbing her. In the end, I decided to leave, but I felt her gaze on me, even for a few moments, as if she was thinking about something unspoken.

Minutes later, I was in another corner of the library, lost in the pages of a book that I wasn't really reading. My thoughts were all revolving around her, around those cold looks, and that harsh way of pushing me away. I knew that this girl wasn't easy... I couldn't stop myself from watching her again.

She was gently placing the book back on the shelf, then turning to leave, without noticing that I was still there. In a moment of weakness, I decided to follow her, not knowing why, but wanting to talk to her again, to understand this mystery that surrounded her.

When she left the library, she walked slowly under the rain, not caring about the raindrops falling on her. Her walk was confident, as if she knew her path well, and I followed her, hesitant between continuing or returning to where I came from. I felt insane; I had never done anything like this in my life.

But something pushed me, maybe that last look that felt like it challenged my weakness. I followed her a few more steps, then finally decided to call out to her: "Lucy!"

She turned to me slowly, with a cold and steady gaze, showing no surprise when she saw me behind her. She stood under the rain, her hair blowing in the wind, but her gaze remained fixed and strong. I couldn't read any emotion in her features; it was as if she expected nothing from me and didn't want to know anything.

I took a deep breath and said with a boldness I didn't expect: "Is it possible for us to meet again?"

She smiled coldly, a smile that carried mockery as if she was laughing at the absurdity of my request. She gave me one last look and said in a calm voice, yet with firm rejection: "You don't know me, and I don't want you to know me. It's better if we forget this meeting here."

She was about to leave, and I, **John**, the young man who had always ignored the meaning of love and romantic stories, found myself clinging to a mysterious desire to extend the conversation further, to create another opportunity to meet her. My heart was pounding insistently, as if my soul had realized that I was in front of something I didn't know I was missing.

Perhaps I did not realize at the time that this complex and awkward meeting was not just a passing incident, but the beginning of a journey, a storm of emotions that would tear me apart and revive me at the same time...

Chapter Two

It is said that kindled souls attract each other, meeting either to complement or to burn... And perhaps I now realize that I have met the soul that might burn me. Days passed after my encounter with **Lucy**, but that moment kept repeating in my mind, replaying itself mercilessly, and I was helpless in forgetting her cold gaze and sharp tone. That girl was like a deep enigma, and despite my efforts to convince myself that she was just a coincidence, my heart would beat every time I remembered her, as if she were a fleeting apparition impossible to forget.

One day, while I was sitting in the usual café, lost in my cup of coffee and my restless thoughts, my friend **Steve** approached me. **Steve** was like a brother, cheerful and spontaneous, always ready to tease me when I seemed distracted.

He said, laughing as he placed a cup of coffee in front of me, "It looks like the dream princess has taken your mind, where are you, **John**?"

I smiled bitterly, then recounted to him my story of meeting **Lucy**, her grim features. He listened attentively, and instead of the mockery I expected, he looked at me seriously and said in a low voice, "You know, they say complicated people are the most attractive... But be careful because attraction doesn't mean you'll understand her or that she'll let you into her world."

I nodded, but I knew I wouldn't be able to retreat. That girl had occupied my thoughts in a way I couldn't explain, and I couldn't ignore her.

The next day, I decided to return to the library, not knowing why, but feeling that I would find her there. I entered the library cautiously, fearing I was mistaken... But I found her there, standing by the shelves, reading quietly as if the whole world had melted into those pages.

I approached slowly, and when she felt my presence, she turned with a surprised look, as if she hadn't expected to see me again.

I said, trying to break the ice with a smile, "It seems I couldn't stick to your advice."

She looked at me coldly and said, "You are stubborn, aren't you?"

I replied, "Maybe, but I want to understand you."

She was silent for a moment, as if pondering my words, then said quietly, "There's nothing you need to understand. I'm just a girl who loves books; I like being here alone."

I felt discouraged, but I couldn't back down.

I pulled up a chair and sat beside her, and said with a slight smile, "Let's start over, as friends. I'm not trying to bother you, let's just talk."

She hesitated a bit but finally agreed with a guarded expression. We started talking about books, and gradually, I found myself knowing more about this mysterious girl, or so I thought...

She told me about her passion for classic books, her love for solitude, and how she hates superficial conversations.

She said, smiling faintly, for the first time since I met her, "I love solitude, I find peace in it. I don't think others understand that."

I replied, "Maybe because you seem very strong, as if you build a wall between you and everyone."

She smiled weakly and said in a low voice, "Sometimes the wall is a protection... You don't know what I've been through."

Her words piqued my curiosity, but I didn't want to press her, so I pointed to a book on the table and we began discussing its author, an attempt to steer the conversation away from personal topics.

In an unexpected moment, a man entered the library. He appeared to be in his thirties, tall, with harsh features and a piercing look. I sensed Lucy's tension as soon as she saw him, as if she was slowly retreating, trying not to attract his attention.

From her distressed look, I understood that they had a troubled history.

I looked at her and asked worriedly, "Do you know him?"

She nodded and said in an embarrassed voice, "This is... Victor."

Victor looked at her with a threatening gaze, then approached us sharply, saying, "Why are you here, Lucy? Isn't escaping enough for you?"

I felt an overwhelming urge to protect Lucy, so I said calmly, trying to appear firm, "Lucy is not alone now."

He stepped back a bit but then said mockingly, "Don't interfere, this is a private matter."

Lucy looked at me with a pleading look, as if asking me not to cause trouble, and then said in a shaky voice, "John, please, let's leave."

We left the library together, with her trembling slightly, but I didn't let go of her hand until we felt safe away from the library.

After she calmed down, she looked at me gratefully and said, "Thank you, I didn't expect to meet you here."

I smiled and said, "Lucy, who is that man? Why did you seem afraid of him?"

She sighed and said in a low voice, "Victor is... a part of my past, a painful past I don't want to remember. A toxic person who tried to control me and dictate my life."

I felt a pang in my heart but tried to show understanding and said gently, "I'm here, no one can bother you as long as I'm around."

She smiled faintly and stepped closer to me, whispering in a soft tone, "For the first time, I feel like I want to trust someone... but I'm afraid, afraid of opening a door I can't close."

I patted her shoulder gently and said, "I won't force you into anything, I'll be here if you need me, anytime."

With this new feeling between us, Lucy felt a sense of security, but I knew deep down that our story wouldn't be easy. Each moment we shared felt like a new heartbeat in my chest, as if I was reborn with every encounter with her.

Those we love are like a mirage; you approach them and reach out, and just when you think you've grasped them, they disappear, leaving you in endless confusion.

The days passed slowly and quietly, but each moment became more complex within me, as if I were walking through a maze of intertwined thoughts and emotions.

My meetings with Lucy became more frequent, and with each meeting, I felt closer to her mysterious world, or so I thought.

Our sessions were a mix of deep silence and few words, each one casting its shadow on the entire situation. **Lucy** tried to keep her distance, but I was not ready to back down.

I remember well how she used to look at me with ambiguous features when I asked her about her constant desire for solitude, about the stories she hid behind those calm eyes.

One of our usual evenings at the café, I was lost in my silence when **Steve**, that loyal friend who notices everything without expressing it, approached us.

He said sarcastically, looking at me and Lucy, "John, anyone who sees your looks would think you are living the tragedy of Romeo and Juliet! What's the matter? Is there a girl in this world who worries you this much?"

I laughed lightly, but **Lucy** didn't seem bothered. She turned to him and said coldly, "Maybe some people are worth worrying about, and sometimes it's better to stay away if you can't understand their story."

Steve looked at her with obvious astonishment and said in a low voice, "Lucy, you might be more complicated than you seem, but I think John deserves some courage from you."

I sensed her silent tension, as Steve's words brought a hint of deep sadness to the surface of her features. She was silent for a while, then she winked at me quietly, as if sending me a message that I would not understand her no matter how much I tried, and that her secrets would remain closed.

A few days later, I met **Lucy** again in the library we used to frequent together, the library that had become our refuge from the noise of the outside world. She was standing between the shelves, looking lost.

I approached her quietly, and when she looked up at me, I noticed that hesitant joy in her eyes.

I asked gently, "Lucy, what did you find here today? It seems your favorite books mean more to you than just words."

She smiled and said softly, "Books are my way of escaping everything. They are a window through which I look out onto a distant world... a world that doesn't require me to be someone else, to hide my pain, or to show my strength."

Her words carried such depth that made me ponder the reality of those walls she built around her. I wanted to know why she wouldn't let me get closer, but I was afraid of seeming like I was burdening her.

Just as we began talking, an unexpected person appeared: **Ethan**, another friend from the distant past who knew my story.

Ethan was a boisterous character who didn't acknowledge boundaries and had his own way of talking to others. He approached us with a small smile on his lips, then looked at me and then at her and said warmly with a sly wink, "Hello, mysterious faces! You know, John, I came by to see how tormented souls look, and here I find myself before them."

Ethan's words elicited a brief laugh from **Lucy**, but it quickly faded, replaced by the familiar silence. Noticing her change in expression, **Ethan** smiled a knowing smile and said, "Lucy, I have a strange feeling that you're hiding something worth a story in one of your books. Or maybe a treasure... do I need a map to decode you?"

Lucy raised her eyebrows in quiet challenge and said, "There may be things that don't need maps to understand, Ethan, but vision, which is rarer than any treasure."

Ethan contemplated her words for a moment, then said quietly, "Maybe, but don't forget that unsolved puzzles keep chasing us, like shadows that never leave."

We all laughed a bit, but that short moment was enough to stir something deep within me. There were signs, ambiguous words, all suggesting that **Lucy** was hiding more than she revealed.

A few days after this encounter, **Lucy** was silent, as if something heavy weighed on her chest. She softly began, as we sat in the park: "John, do you know what it means to be afraid of your past?"

Her tone surprised me, but I tried to show her support and said cautiously, "Lucy, the past is part of us, but we shouldn't let it rule our entire lives."

She looked at me with a deep, heavy gaze, then said firmly, "There are people from the past who don't leave easily, even when we try to escape. I told you about **Victor**, but I didn't tell you everything."

I felt tense, a mix of sadness and anger.

She spoke slowly, as if bleeding with each word: "**Victor** wasn't just someone from the past... he was someone who controlled my life. He loved me obsessively, wanted me the way he wanted, not as I am. I tried to leave him, but I didn't have enough strength. He was manipulative, making me feel like I owed him everything."

She paused for a moment, then continued in a trembling voice: "When I decided to leave, he decided to follow me. I thought I was free, but I still feel his breath chasing me, like a shadow that won't leave."

I felt anger and jealousy at the same time, gently holding her hand, trying to reassure her: "Lucy, you're here now, no one can hurt you anymore. I'm with you, and I'll stay by your side."

She listened to my words, but I knew the barriers between us hadn't been broken yet.

She was silent for a bit, then whispered with a hint of hope: "John, I don't know if I can trust anyone. Sometimes I feel like a shadow looking for an impossible safety."

At that moment, I realized that the soul in front of me wasn't seeking love but seeking protection. Seeking the tenderness that could drive away the ghosts of the past.

But before I could respond, **Victor** appeared suddenly, as if part of a nightmare decided to peek through the folds of reality. His features were tense, his eyes filled with anger and hatred. He stood in front of us, glaring at me with a threatening look as if warning me.

He said harshly, "Lucy, why are you trying to escape from me? Haven't you understood yet that you belong to me alone?"

I felt a boiling rage inside and stood between them, trying to show firmness in front of him.

I said in a strong tone, "Victor, she doesn't want you in her life. Leave her alone."

He laughed mockingly and said, "Who do you think you are to interfere in something that doesn't concern you? This is a matter between me and her."

For the first time, **Lucy** looked at him with a defiant gaze and said with a firmness I hadn't seen from her before, "Victor, it's over. I am not yours. I won't let you control my life again."

Victor gave her a threatening look, turned his back, and walked away... but I felt this confrontation was just the beginning, the start of a long struggle with the ghosts that still haunt her.

I stood by her side, holding her hand, as if telling her that I would stay with her, no matter the thorns awaiting us.

I whispered to her, "Lucy, I won't let anyone hurt you. I'll stay here until the end."

Chapter Three

In love, we may meet in moments of happiness, but true honesty lies in those times when challenges test our hearts and reveal how sincere our love is. Many days passed after the confrontation with **Victor**, and gradually, I began to notice a change in **Lucy**'s eyes. They became warmer.

Despite the ghosts of the past still haunting her, I could see that my presence with her alleviated some of the pain that had weighed her down for so long.

One day, I met **Lucy** at the café we used to meet in. She was sitting in a quiet corner, sipping her coffee slowly. She was lost in her thoughts, staring out the window as if searching for an answer to a troubling question.

I sat beside her in silence, feeling that she was waiting for something from me without uttering a word.

I said quietly, "Lucy, I know there are many things between us that haven't been said yet, but I'm here to listen, only when you're ready."

She let out a small sigh, then turned to me and said, "John, there are many things inside me, things I can't easily get rid of. But with you, I feel like I can be myself."

I listened to her, my heart pounding, and I realized that I was beginning to see new aspects of her. She was honest, gently holding my hands in hers, and I said sincerely, "Lucy, you are not alone in this battle. I won't let you face the past on your own."

She smiled a silent thank you and said, "John, there are things from the past I haven't told you about yet. My relationship with **Victor** was more than just a finished love story... it was a series of chains that I felt I would never break free from."

She paused for a moment as if gathering her thoughts, then continued, "When I left him, I decided to start a new life, but he wouldn't allow me. He kept chasing me, sending me threatening messages. Sometimes I wake up from sleep feeling his presence, watching me from afar. I couldn't sleep peacefully for months."

I felt anger rising within me, but I tried to remain calm and answered her honestly, "Lucy, I won't let this past haunt you anymore. I am here, with you, and I won't let anyone hurt you."

She looked at me with gratitude, as if she had found in me the security she had long missed.

In that moment, I decided to take her away from the heavy memories, so I suggested we take a walk in the park we both loved. That park had large trees and quiet streams, and its atmosphere was enough to remove any fatigue from our tired souls.

During our walk, **Lucy** began to regain her vitality. She laughed at old stories I told her about my childhood and how I stumbled in every attempt to climb a tree. She laughed from her heart, as if the sadness she had carried had dissipated, if only for a moment.

As we walked through the park, an old man selling flowers passed by. I approached him and bought a bouquet of white flowers, then handed them to **Lucy** with a light smile, saying, "White flowers symbolize peace... just as I wish your life to be from now on."

She took the flowers and looked at me deeply, as if trying to read beyond my words. She said gently, "John, in my life, I have met many people, but I have never found someone who sees behind the barriers as you do."

Her words ignited an indescribable feeling within me. I didn't know that one day I would become part of her complex world, but she was everything I wanted, everything my heart, which had long sought a warm refuge, needed.

While we were talking, **Steve** called and insisted that we join him for dinner that night. We agreed, and during our gathering, the atmosphere was filled with fun, and **Steve** tried in every possible way to bring laughter to our faces.

At one point, **Steve** said jokingly, "John, did you know I have never seen someone so obsessed with a girl this quickly as you are! I almost think your heart is in her hands."

Lucy laughed shyly, but I couldn't let the opportunity pass, so I said honestly, "A dream I've been searching for my entire life."

Steve looked at me seriously and said, "You know the road won't be easy, right? There are many things that might stand in your way."

I replied firmly, "I understand that, but I won't leave her no matter the cost. I've spent my whole life waiting for something like this. How can I retreat after I've found it?"

The evening passed quickly, and **Lucy** returned to her apartment while I went home, filled with thoughts and reflections about the future. I knew **Victor** wasn't the only challenge we might face, but I was ready to endure anything for her.

As I pondered the details of our day, I received a message from **Lucy** saying, "John, I feel like I'm living between a dream and reality, but I'm afraid of losing everything... I'm afraid that the safety I feel with you will disappear."

I replied, "Lucy, I will protect you from every fear. All you need to do is trust me, and we will find our way together."

That night marked a new beginning between us, a promise to be the security she had long missed. Every moment with her was a moment that stole my sleep, every thought about her filled my heart with the fear of being away from her.

Life began to flow again as if time had finally decided to give us a break from its struggles. The days passed, and I found myself standing between two moments... the moment I lived with **Lucy**, and another where her memories returned to darkness, causing chaos within me.

Although I tried to be her support, I felt that something in her heart hadn't healed yet. As days went by, **Lucy** became closer, but she always distanced herself at certain moments, as if she was afraid to approach the edge of fear.

I realized that behind those sad smiles lay a mysterious being, not yet ready to come into the light. I wondered about the things she was hiding from me, but I also knew that I needed time for her to understand what was in her heart.

One day, I was sitting in my office when my phone rang. It was **Steve**.

He said in a serious voice, "John, I need you to come now. There's something I need to talk to you about."

I replied quickly, "What's going on?"

He said, "I can't explain over the phone. Just come quickly," and then he hung up.

I couldn't pinpoint what was troubling **Steve**, but I felt something unsettling.

I rushed over, and when I arrived, I found **Steve** sitting on a chair in the café, fiddling with his coffee cup with a distant look in his eyes.

I asked anxiously, "What's the matter, Steve?"

He looked at me with a hazy smile and said, "I know you'll feel confused, but I need to tell you something."

I responded, "What is it?"

At that moment, he took a deep breath, as if the words were torturing his tongue, and then said, "I've discovered that **Victor** hasn't forgotten about **Lucy**. He is now planning to take revenge on her."

I froze in place, feeling like the sky had fallen on my head.

Victor? The man **Lucy** was trying to escape from? I felt a wave of anguish flood my heart. How could this person chase her again? Wasn't he supposed to leave her alone?

I asked in a trembling voice, "How do you know this?"

Steve replied, "I heard some talk from mutual friends. He's planning to get back into her life, and he won't be happy if he finds out we're trying to protect her."

I stood in silence for a long time, feeling fear creeping inside me. **Lucy**, who had become an integral part of my life, was about to face her past again, and I felt powerless to protect her.

The fear for her heart pained me more than anything else. But I was determined not to let her go through this alone.

I went to **Lucy** that night; the weather was cold, and the wind was howling through the trees outside. When I saw her, her eyes were lost in the void.

She looked at me with a light smile, but I couldn't hide the worry that filled my eyes.

I said firmly, "Lucy, we need to talk."

She replied calmly, "What's the matter?"

I said, "I've found out that **Victor** will return. He's planning to take revenge on you. And I won't let him hurt you again."

She was silent for a moment, as if she was absorbing what I had said. Then she looked at me and said in a low voice, "I knew he would never leave me alone. But I didn't expect him to threaten me this way. I don't want you to get involved in my problems."

I reached out my hand and gently held hers, saying, "I won't leave you alone, Lucy. We'll face him together. He won't be able to harm us."

At that moment, I saw in her eyes a look of gratitude and sorrow at the same time, as if she finally realized that there was someone who could be her true support, someone who would stay with her despite the darkness and fears. Her heart was breathing life again...

But I knew the challenges wouldn't end here. On the contrary, we were just beginning to dive into the depths of the game **Victor** had chosen, and we might not be fully prepared for what would happen in the coming days.

We talked for a long time, and **Lucy** seemed more at ease after we discussed everything. But I fully realized that the shadows that had been chasing her for years wouldn't disappear that easily. I saw in her depths that deep fear that couldn't be eradicated, something that required a lot of patience and time from us.

That night, when I said goodbye to **Lucy**, I said to her, "I will always be here, and I will protect you from everything. You are part of my life now, and I won't leave you."

She smiled, but the smile carried a lot of pain. She said, "John, I don't want to disappoint you, but I'm afraid of being a burden on you."

I replied confidently, "You are not a burden, Lucy. You are the reason that makes me believe this world can be more beautiful."

As she closed the door behind her, I felt something strange, as if I stood on the edge of something very big, something that would change everything in our lives. All I knew then was that I couldn't go back.

Sometimes, the past is the closest ghost, appearing to us in a moment of weakness, forcing us to face what we thought we had buried far away...

As the days went by, my relationship with **Lucy** gradually transformed from a desire to protect and care for her to a deeper connection, one filled with thoughts about the future and dreams of a shared life, but also with a constant fear of the ghost of the past.

One day, while walking in the park, we heard a familiar sound, it was the sound of unfamiliar laughter from afar, approaching slowly. It seemed to be coming from a distant place, but it deepened in our minds until I realized that the sound was more familiar to **Lucy** than I had imagined. She suddenly stopped, looked at me with eyes full of terror, and said, "Victor... he's here."

I turned to the direction she pointed, and there he stood, **Victor**, the man **Lucy** had tried to escape from for years. He stood with strange confidence and a defiant look. Anger surged within me, but I composed myself. It was as if **Victor** sensed my weakness in front of him, and he smiled mockingly and approached us.

He looked at me with a sarcastic gaze and said in a cold voice, "John, isn't it? It seems that **Lucy** still clings to my memories, even if not with her hands, then with her spirit."

I replied with restrained anger, "Victor, leave her alone. She is no longer a part of your life."

Victor laughed softly and said, "Oh, my friend, we don't choose to leave something or own it that easily. Sometimes we remain part of someone else's life despite ourselves, isn't that right, Lucy?"

Lucy stood beside me in silence, her eyes wide with fear, as if she were a little girl facing a ghost from the past. I held her hand to calm her, realizing then how heavily the past weighed on her. She looked at me and said in a choked voice, "John, I don't want to go through this pain again. I've been through so much, and I need you by my side now more than ever."

I turned towards **Victor** and said firmly, "Withdraw from her life. Your role here is over."

Victor turned his face towards me and said coldly, "Do you really think I will leave her? John, love is not a game that ends and is put away, but a vortex, swirling around us until we lose everything."

Victor left, leaving behind the burden of heavy memories, as if the air around us had become heavier. We walked together, and I tried to process what had just happened, how the past could return to disrupt our stability in moments.

That night, we went to the café. I sat beside her, and our silence weighed heavily on the place. She cried silently, while I took her hand in mine, trying to reassure her. She said in a hoarse voice, "John, I'm sorry... I didn't want you to be part of this mess."

I answered calmly, "Lucy, I'm here because I want to be part of your life, whether it's filled with problems or happiness. I will always be by your side."

She looked at me with eyes filled with pain and gratitude, as if my words had brought her comfort.

She said, "I've always been strong, but now I feel I need someone to protect me, stand by my side... and that person is you."

At that moment, I felt like we were living in a world of our own, where no one could disturb its tranquility. But there were signs scattered here and there, making me feel that this world might not last long.

A few days later, I received a call from **Steve**, my close friend who knew much about **Lucy's** past and **Victor's** threats.

He said in a serious voice, "John, listen, I've learned some things that might help you. **Victor** doesn't intend to stop at verbal threats. It could turn into a real threat."

I felt a lump in my throat and answered anxiously, "Steve, what do you mean?"

He replied seriously, "Victor is not someone who gives up easily. You need to be careful and protect Lucy with all you can."

I realized that things had become more complicated than I had imagined and that I had to prepare for the worst. I was ready to endure anything for **Lucy**, but I didn't know how far **Victor** would go.

The following night, I was sitting with **Lucy**, talking about our dreams and the life we wanted to build together, far from all those painful memories. I said to her, "Lucy, don't worry, I will be here to protect you. I will stay by your side no matter what happens."

She looked at me with a sad smile and said, "John, I wish it were that simple. I feel helpless in the face of all this, like I'm running in an endless whirlwind."

I smiled at her and said calmly, "When you're with me, you'll feel safe. I won't let anything disrupt our lives."

As I was speaking, she moved closer to me, rested her head on my shoulder, and whispered in a faint voice, "I just want to forget everything and start anew with you."

It was as if she was seeking refuge from all her fears...

Chapter Four

Sometimes, we meet someone not because we need them, but because our destiny demands that we discover ourselves through them.

As the night covered the city's sky like a cloak, many questions gathered in my heart that I couldn't answer. How can a relationship become so fragile? How can memories become sharp knives that wound me every time I remember them? **Lucy** was always on my mind; I couldn't ignore her complex feelings that I couldn't understand.

I wanted to be the person who fills her heart, to be the one who stands by her in facing her deepest fears.

One rainy day, I met **Lucy** in an unusual place. She was sitting in a small café on the outskirts of the city, where few people passed by. The place was quiet, as if time had stopped there, leaving just us.

I approached her and sat in silence, our eyes meeting without saying a word. After a few moments, she smiled faintly, indicating that there was something on her heart.

She finally said, "Do you know, John? I think I can't run away from myself anymore."

I looked at her with concern, "What do you mean?"

She spoke as if the words were coming from her depths, "I mean... I can't run away from the past, from **Victor**. No matter how much I try to start anew, he comes back to me. He's like a shadow that never leaves me."

Lucy had always been the focus of my attention, but in that moment, I felt like I couldn't help her, even though I was beside her. I searched for a way to reassure her, but the words were insufficient. I wanted to tell her that I would always be there, but I felt that in the depths of her heart, there was a deep, lonely void that only she could fill.

The rain was pouring down the window, and everything seemed blurry around us.

I whispered, "Lucy, why don't we leave together? Why don't we escape from all this? We go to a faraway place, start anew. No past, no **Victor**, no one."

She looked at me for a while, then replied in a calm voice, "John, I want to believe you. I want to live this moment, but there's a part of me that won't let me leave everything behind. There was a time when I thought I would be happy, but... the closer I get to you, the more I feel like I'm falling into a bigger trap."

Moments of silence followed. As her words seeped into my heart, I felt she was still spinning in a whirlpool she didn't know how to get out of. I wanted to be the rope that pulls her out of that whirlpool, but I was facing resistance from her heart itself.

For her, separation was like an old pain she lived with but couldn't rid herself of.

In that moment, I moved closer and held her hand, saying, "If you can't escape the past, come with me to the future. Let's build something new together, something untouched by the hands of time."

Her eyes were filled with tears, but she looked at me as if finding a glimmer of lost hope in my words. She whispered weakly, "I want you, John. But my fear is greater than anything else. I'm afraid that if I let you get close, I'll lose everything."

Hearts race, but each one carries a wound, and each of us wishes that time could heal these wounds.

The next day, the rain was still falling, but I felt a pressure in my chest. There was something unnatural in the air, as if the entire world was waiting for something big. **Lucy** avoided talking about **Victor** and distanced herself every time I got closer.

I found myself standing in the middle of a bustling city, nothing mattered except understanding what was happening in her heart. I kept thinking about her words repeatedly, trying to figure out what made her hold back. Why were her eyes filled with fear?

Then, one night, as I was sitting in my study, I received a call from **Steve**.

He said in a serious tone, "John, there's something you need to know about Victor. He doesn't just stop at making threats."

I asked, wondering about the severity of what he was saying, "What do you mean?"

Steve said, "I've received information. **Victor** is planning something bigger than just following her. He wants to make her choose between him and you, and he'll do anything to achieve his goal."

I was shocked again, feeling like I was at another turning point in my life, one I wasn't prepared for. **Victor** was just the beginning, and now we were sinking into a big game whose rules we didn't know.

As I thought about how to handle this situation, I remembered **Lucy's** words: "I don't want to disappoint you."

The next day, I decided to meet her in the place she had loved for so long, where she used to find some peace. She was sitting on a bench in the park, her eyes gazing at the distant horizon.

I approached her slowly, and when she felt my presence, she said in a low voice, "John, I'm scared. I'm scared I'll lose everything again."

I sat beside her and said, "I won't let you down, Lucy. I won't let you lose everything. If there's one person who can protect you, it's me. We're together now, and I won't leave you."

Then, looking into her eyes, I whispered, "I won't let anything tear us apart."

At that moment, the rain had stopped, and I knew these moments were just the beginning of an upcoming confrontation. Sometimes, time creates a void within us, which love fills, but fear disrupts its serenity.

Lucy's heart was beating silently, and every time we looked at each other, understanding seeped through our eyes as if we were reading each other's thoughts. But I knew she was resisting, resisting a truth she wasn't ready to face yet.

This was the moment I felt I wasn't just someone trying to save her, but I was the one drifting with her in a whirlpool of endless past and memories. Day after day, **Victor's** eyes haunted us, and every time we tried to find an escape, the past returned to block our way.

Victor wasn't just a threat; he was a weapon used against us, driven by his spite and refusal to move on. One day, while we were waiting at the café where we spent most of our time together, another person walked in.

His eyes pierced through me as if trying to uncover what was inside me, and he laughed quietly. His name was **Steve**, and he knew everything about the shared past between **Lucy** and **Victor**.

Steve said with a light smile but with worry in his eyes that he couldn't hide, "John, we can hide in this place forever, but you know **Victor** doesn't know surrender. He doesn't back down."

I didn't answer at first. The internal voice was screaming at me, but I just wanted to put an end to this tension that was increasing day by day. Even **Lucy** was trying to appear steadfast, but I could see how fear was creeping into her heart little by little.

Lucy said, her voice low, "I want to be with you, John, but the past doesn't stop chasing me."

Her words were like a stab in the heart because they meant more than I initially understood. They meant she was carrying a heavy burden, a burden that no one else could carry for her, not even me. She was still missing something within herself, something I couldn't fill.

Can a person truly heal from their wounds? Or do we just learn to live with them? I thought about her words as I watched her eyes, and I couldn't help but wonder what was really occupying her mind.

Then, suddenly, the silence was broken by **Victor's** entrance, approaching with confident steps. He seemed calm, but his eyes held something dark within them. Finally, he stood before us and said, directing his words straight at me, "John, I believe **Lucy** hasn't told you everything yet."

I felt something heavy drop on my chest, knowing at that moment that I was on the verge of discovering something I didn't want to know. **Lucy** avoided looking at him while he stared into my eyes with contempt.

The silence was louder than words.

Victor, sensing my shock, said, "You don't know what it's like to live with this person, John. You don't know how terrifying it is to be a victim of a draining relationship. **Lucy** hides the truth from you, and you think you can save her. But you can't."

Lucy murmured without lifting her eyes, "You don't know anything about me, Victor. Leave."

But **Victor** didn't flinch; on the contrary, he said with clear sarcasm, "You can't run away from me. As long as you think you can move on, you'll discover that the past always returns to present you with a hard choice. I'm here to remind you of that."

At that moment, conflicting emotions overwhelmed me. I wanted to protect **Lucy**, to tell her that everything would be alright, but I knew fear was binding her. What **Victor** said was painfully true. The past doesn't leave easily, and every time we think we distance ourselves from it, we discover that it traps us more.

I asked him, "What do you want, Victor? Do you think your threats will change anything?"

Victor smiled lightly, then said, "I'm here to make you both see the truth. The truth **Lucy** refuses to acknowledge."

Then, suddenly, something unexpected happened. Another man entered the café, carrying a large file in his hands. His eyes were full of tension, and he seemed to be in a hurry. He stopped in front of **Victor** and said firmly, "It's time for reckoning, Victor."

The man approached us slowly, then lifted the file and handed it to **Victor**. **Victor** opened it quickly, his eyes widening in shock. The file contained old documents, photos, and evidence of suspicious activities.

The man said in a harsh tone, "This is the truth you've been hiding from **Lucy**, Victor."

I was struck by silence again. I didn't know what was happening, but what was in this file was something bigger than his previous threats. It was something that threatened **Lucy's** life and everything I thought I knew about the past. This was the decisive moment that would reveal everything to us.

What was the truth **Victor** was hiding? Was the past more unjust than we imagined?

As I watched this emotional and real struggle, I realized our lives were about to change forever. Sometimes, we don't need answers; what we need is the strength to live with the questions.

Everything in that moment was boiling inside me.

What did all this mean? What did it mean for another person to stand before me, laden with documents that could change everything in my life? I never expected things to reach this point.

Victor wasn't just someone in **Lucy's** life; he was a looming shadow, chasing us every time we tried to distance ourselves from the past. While **Lucy** sat at the table, seemingly unable to move her hand or speak, I felt a kind of helplessness squeezing my heart. Everything seemed out of reach.

Victor, who didn't know the meaning of mercy, smiled a malicious smile as he opened the file in front of us. The man who brought it remained standing, observing us all as if this moment was the beginning of the end of a long game.

"What does this mean?" I wondered in a low voice, watching **Victor** quickly flip through the pages, then pause to stare at **Lucy**. It felt like a scene from an old movie, where the person remains at the peak of their emotions, trapped between the past and the future.

Victor raised his eyes and took a deep breath, then said, "These documents, **Lucy**, this is the truth you're hiding from yourself. You can't escape this now."

His words hit **Lucy** like a thunderbolt, causing her to recoil as if the truth were a massive wall pressing down on her. Her eyes filled with tears, and when she tried to speak, it seemed like the words were stuck in her throat, unable to come out.

"You don't know anything, **Victor**." **Lucy** finally said in a very quiet voice, as if she were speaking to herself more than to him. "You don't know what I've been through, or what we've been through together."

But **Victor** wasn't listening. He was entirely focused on the documents in front of him, seemingly enjoying watching **Lucy** suffer. "I know everything, **Lucy**. Everything about you. Everything about those days you tried to forget."

Then he looked at me and said, "And you, **John**, if you knew what I know, you wouldn't be sitting here so calmly."

I felt like I was watching a play, with each event accelerating before me, and its complications increasing. I was thinking about everything, every moment that had passed between **Lucy** and me. Fear filled my heart, but there was something else pressing on me. A feeling of insecurity, not yet knowing the whole truth, and these documents could be a turning point.

"What do you want from me?" I finally asked **Victor**, having lost my temper but knowing I needed to stay calm. "Do you want to destroy everything? Do you want us to live in the shadow of the past?"

Victor laughed shortly, then said, "No, **John**. I just want you to understand one thing: **Lucy** is not yours. She was never anyone's before, and she won't be anyone's after now."

At that moment, **Lucy's** eyes fixed on him, and silence took over the place.

Victor's words were like a bullet to her heart, as if she knew that everything was changing before her eyes. But before she spoke, it was that decisive moment that could turn everything upside down. "Nothing in life is worth sacrificing for unless it holds a heart worthy of love."

And **Lucy**, at that moment, realized something new. She looked at me, then at **Victor**, and there was a storm of conflicting emotions between us, but she finally said in a determined voice, "I'm tired of running. I'm tired of hiding the truth."

She took a deep breath, as if she were preparing to dive into the sea. Then she looked at me and said, "John, there were things in my life you can't understand. **Victor** was part of it, and part of the pain I can't bear anymore."

Her words fell from her like leaves in the autumn. "I've made many mistakes, and I know that." She added, wiping her tears, "But I don't want to be a part of the past anymore."

As she smiled sadly, I realized I was in a place I didn't expect. I thought I could fix everything. But in the end, what was happening was bigger than me, bigger than my ability to control it.

Lucy said in a steady voice, "John, if you truly love me, let me go."

This was the final plea. It was a silent request; one I wasn't ready to hear. But I knew that sometimes the truth requires us to let go of the things we love the most.

There was something big on the horizon, something I knew would change our lives forever. "I can't leave you," I whispered, but I knew deep down that I might be the last person in her life.

As that moment ended, I realized everything would change after this meeting. There was something deep and dark in those papers that fell before us, something we wouldn't be able to escape.

At that moment, the truth began to reveal itself... Was **Lucy** ready to face what was in the past? And was I ready to face everything that would follow?

Chapter Five

Sometimes, we find our safety in the farthest place from everything we've known... We shed the cloak of the past and are born anew.

Those last days in the city felt like a struggle between the past and the future. We spent them bidding farewell to friends who shared our laughter and secrets, saying goodbye as if we carried a piece of each of them in our hearts, taking them with us on a journey that might be without return.

Lucy was silent the whole time, her eyes filled with the exhaustion of the past years, as if she were bidding farewell not just to her friends but to her old self. When we stood at the airport gate, there was a long moment of silence between us. **Steve**, his voice faltering as he tried to hide his tears, said,

"Wherever you go, you will always be a part of us... Seek happiness, and don't forget that there are hearts waiting for your news always."

His words left a spark of hope in our hearts, but they also marked the end of a significant chapter in our lives.

We arrived in a new homeland, a place far away from everything, as if we had returned to square one, where nothing was familiar, and no one was waiting for us.

We chose a small town overlooking the sea, like an oasis of tranquility that had been waiting for us for a long time. Life here resembled a beautiful scene from a novel, with small, aligned houses, the colors of blooming flowers on window sills, and old shops telling stories from other days. It felt like we were seeking refuge not to hide but to start a new journey.

We chose a small apartment overlooking the sea, its balcony facing an endless horizon. This place, despite its simplicity, was a sanctuary for us, a part of a dream we had never dreamed of before. Every morning, we woke up to the sound of waves, as if the sea was greeting us, saying, "You have arrived at safety."

On the first morning after our arrival, as **Lucy** gazed at the city from the window, I asked her in a soft voice, "What do you think of this place? Do you find your comfort here?"

She smiled tenderly and answered with hope-filled words, "Here... here I want to forget everything. I want too just live... just us."

Her word "us" carried all the love.

Our days in that city resembled pages from a beautiful novel. We began to wander through the small markets, getting to know the strange faces, the people who looked at us as if we were a new story in their quiet town.

We were looking for work to fill our days and support us in building this new dream. One day, we stumbled upon a small café on the edge of the beach, run by a kind old man named **Robert**.

Robert's eyes did not betray his old age; he laughed heartily and spoke enthusiastically about his youthful days, as if he found in us a new opportunity for joy.

We introduced ourselves, and he said with a wide smile, "Why don't you both work with me here? This place needs new spirits, young hands, and pure dreams."

Lucy and I felt that this offer was a gift from fate, as if life here was slowly opening its doors to us.

Every day, we worked with **Robert** at the café. **Lucy** prepared coffee and tea, quickly learning his special recipes, and she became adept at making the coffee that **Robert**'s loyal customers loved.

As for me, I helped him with everything, from cleaning tables to preparing food. Sometimes, I stood behind the piano in the corner of the café, playing simple pieces that made the café's visitors smile.

In the evenings, after the café closed its doors, we would return to our balcony, look at the sea, and talk about our dreams—dreams we hadn't dared to think about before. We dreamed of opening our own café, a small place where we could welcome people with warmth and smiles, just as **Robert** had done for us.

"**John**, if we could build this place here, a place that would be a refuge just like we found in this new homeland," **Lucy** said once, her smile illuminating her face with a special glow.

I gently held her hand and replied, "We will achieve that, **Lucy**. Everything is possible here, far from everything."

Those little moments between us made me see the world differently, as if I didn't need anything else but her presence beside me.

Life here was simple, but it was full of joy. Time passed, and we began to form relationships in this quiet town. We received dinner invitations from customers who became our friends, each carrying a different story, a new face, seeing us as a young couple who found peace in this place, as if they saw a part of hope in us.

In simplicity lies beauty, and in small details, deep stories are hidden.

Lucy moved through life here with freedom, her smile reflecting the beauty of her heart, her personality growing stronger and brighter with each passing day. In some evenings, she wore a white dress and tied her hair with a blue ribbon, looking like a little angel walking through the café, laughing with the children who came with their families, exchanging jokes with **Robert**, who had become like a father to us.

Over time, my relationship with **Lucy** deepened. We felt that our love had become stronger. Love between us was no longer just feelings but a language spoken through our actions and the details of our daily lives. Every time I looked at **Lucy**, I felt that life had given me a new chance, a chance to live love, a chance to live.

One day, while we were sitting on the balcony, talking about everything and watching the stars, **Lucy** looked at me with a calm smile and said, "**John**, I'm happy, so happy that I don't need anything else... Here, I feel like I've been born again."

Her words penetrated my heart as if telling me that everything had changed for the better. Every time I look at you, I find in your eyes what life could not grant me.

The days passed with a beloved slowness, like a warm breeze, enveloping **Lucy** and **John** with a feeling they had never known before, as if they were living a love story outside of time, unbound by limits and unchallenged by circumstances.

Every morning, **Lucy** started her day by tending to the flowers that decorated the place. She chose white flowers and carefully scattered them on the tables, as if she wanted to infuse the place with a piece of her soul. She made sure every corner was beautiful, reflecting her and **John**'s dream.

One sunny morning, while **Lucy** was arranging small books on the café's shelves, I came in carrying two cups of hot coffee. I placed one in front of her and said with a smile, "I still believe you have a magical ability. How do you make the place speak your name and reflect your spirit?"

She answered with a shy smile, "And you, haven't you noticed that you've become a part of everything here? I see you in every detail, in every glance, even in the aroma of the coffee."

Love isn't just a promise in words; it's a sincere presence in every small detail that shows we are building a world that resembles us together.

As days went by, I planned a special surprise for **Lucy** on one summer night.

I waited until the sun had set, then quietly closed the café, turned off the lights, took her hand, and we walked together. We slowly climbed up to the rooftop, where I had set up a simple table surrounded by soft candles and scattered flowers, with gentle music filling the air.

When **Lucy** reached the rooftop and saw the setup, she gasped in surprise. She laughed and said, "John! What have you been planning without telling me?"

I smiled and looked at her, "To see you radiant and happy, all this is for you."

She smiled with love and sat in front of me, looking at me lovingly. I took her hand in mine and said, "Do you know? I feel like we're in another world, and nothing outside this moment matters. In your eyes, I found what I was looking for, and found myself near you, as if you were my mirror."

Silence prevailed for a moment, but we didn't need words. The silence spoke for us, carrying our stories that our hearts knew. **Lucy** gazed at the stars and smiled, saying, "I've always dreamed of a faraway place, where there's nothing but peace and love. Today, I live it with you."

I answered with a smile, "We will create this place, and we won't let it slip away. This moment is my promise to you; we will never give up on our dream."

That night, we sat for hours, talking about other dreams that might come, and the days ahead.

Chapter Six

You are the reason for every beautiful moment I live, with you.

The sun was setting in the sky as I continued preparing my surprise for her. I felt an indescribable sensation in my heart, a feeling that this day was the moment I had long dreamed of, and finally, it was time to make it happen.

This was not just an ordinary day; it was the beginning of a new chapter in our lives. A chapter I had meticulously planned for, hoping it would be a special moment for her.

I had always known how much **Lucy** loved small cafés, those that emitted the aroma of coffee and had a calm and comfortable atmosphere in their corners. I knew she preferred places that were lively but quiet enough to feel like her own world.

I thought of something that suited her, something that reflected the beauty of her spirit, and I decided that this café would be my gift to her. For a few weeks, I worked tirelessly with the team. Ideas raced through my mind, intertwining between the desire to show her how special she was and ensuring everything was in its perfect place.

We chose a design that reflected her style, with the calm colors she loved and simple yet tasteful decorations. The café walls were adorned with the books she loved and flowers, memories of the moments we had shared since we first met, and the words we had exchanged with each other.

As I put the final touches in place, the grand surprise was nearing. I had decided to name it "Lucy's Café." It was more than just a name; it was a message, an expression of everything her presence in my life meant.

This café was more than just a place to spend time; it was a symbol of our love; of the life we had built together.

Then the awaited day came. I had invited her to meet a friend of mine at this new café...

I didn't tell her anything; I wanted her surprise to be complete and to see her reaction when she found the place I had been working on. When she walked in, the amazement in her eyes was evident.

She paused for a moment, her eyes scanning the place, then moved to the sign bearing the name.

"**John**..." she whispered, then slowly walked towards the café.

She stood in front of the sign that said "Lucy's Café," her eyes barely believing what they were seeing. She looked at me, as if to confirm that I wasn't joking. "Is this... is this a new café?"

I smiled as I approached her.

I took her hand gently and said, "Yes, my love. This is your place. I'm here just to give you something that reflects your beauty and spirit... This café, and its name, is an expression of a part of what you mean to me. You are more beautiful than all the colors, than all the details. This café is just the beginning."

Her eyes sparkled with tears, as if words had lost their ability to express. She stood there, not knowing what to say.

Then, after a moment of silence, she smiled deeply, as if everything in her heart had faded away, leaving only this place and this moment, which encapsulated all the meanings of love and giving.

I felt as if I could see all of life embodied in her eyes.

I had dreamed of this day many times, and now, everything was coming true. And that place, with its beauty and simplicity, was a testament to our endless love.

Lucy wandered around the café with slow steps, examining every corner. She touched the walls as if feeling the hidden memories in every nook.

She smiled, moving between the tables, each step carrying a bit of joy.

At that moment, I remembered all the times I had been with her in other cafés, noticing how she observed everything with an artist's eye, contemplating the small details of the place.

Suddenly, she said to me in a quiet voice, "You really amazed me, **John**. How did you know this is exactly what I wanted?"

I answered with a smile full of love, "Because I know you better than myself. I know that this place, with all its details, reflects you. It reflects your beauty and spirit."

I held her hand tightly and made her sit next to me on one of the small chairs in the corner.

The aroma of coffee, the books, and the soft music that filled the place made everything perfect.

We sat there; everything was complete.

This place, this moment, everything in it seemed as if the entire universe had been waiting for it.

I told her about all the details I had taken care of, about the flowers she had carefully chosen, the books she loved to read that I had placed on the shelves, and all the details that concerned us.

She smiled every time I talked about something small, we had experienced together in our lives.

Then, in that moment, I realized that this café was not just a physical place. It was a reflection of our love that started small and then grew to become something great.

It was a new beginning together, in this place that bore **Lucy**'s name, filled with the love and memories we had built together.

You don't know how much it means to me to see you happy. That day, everything seemed different.

The air itself was throbbing with hope, and the sun was shining in a new way, as if life was waiting for us to move forward, to start a new chapter, a chapter unlike any other.

I sat in the new café, watching **Lucy** as she roamed the place with her bright eyes, as if rediscovering every corner, every nook.

A place that had become more than just a project; it was a dream that had come true. Everything had been designed especially for her; from the colors she chose for the walls to the furniture that was simple yet elegant. The name of the café shone in golden letters on the wall: "Lucy."

It wasn't easy for me to hide my happiness as I saw how our ideas had turned into a tangible reality before our eyes.

How everything began to materialize after we had been dreaming about it all this time. There was something in her eyes, something greater than happiness, something indescribable.

It was as if her heart was narrating every moment of love in this small space that had become our home.

"**John**... I can't believe it! This café... it's more beautiful than anything I had imagined." **Lucy** said in her gentle voice, and the words came from the depths of her heart.

I couldn't resist, and I smiled a big smile.

"All this is for you," I replied, feeling that every word that came out of my mouth carried with it a promise that we would always be together, building this future with our own hands. "Every corner here, every detail, every moment, is ours."

She then came closer to me, and with her hand, which was trembling slightly with emotion, she held my hand.

"You know how much I love you, **John**, but you've done something I can't describe."

As the words fell from her like pearls, I felt something strange inside me, as if the love between us had become greater than everything.

Nothing can separate us now because we are together, in this place that bears her name, that we started together.

"It's a beginning, **Lucy**," I said as I met her gaze. "Not just for the café, but for a new life, for a dream we started together."

She smiled with love, then said, "But you don't need to buy me anything to know that we are together."

"But you deserve everything, and more." My words were sincere because I realized how much she had been a partner in every step, in every idea, in every plan. She was the endless love.

Now the place had become more than just a space of walls and furniture. It had become ours, the two of us, the dream that had come true.

Then, at that moment, we decided to celebrate our first day in the new café.

We sat together, she and I, and drank a cup of coffee. In this place that had become ours, within this dream that had become a reality. But we had only one thing in our hands: hope for the future and the happiness that would not be complete without her.

"I don't want to go anywhere, I don't want to leave you," I said as I sipped the coffee, my heart beating fast, as if I were telling her everything that was stirring inside me.

"And I too, I don't want to leave you, I love you," **Lucy** replied in a low voice, looking into my eyes with eyes full of love.

As time went by, the café began to take its true shape.

It became more than just a place we worked in. We had memories filling the place.

And customers began to come day after day, walking between the tables as if they had entered another world, a world filled with peace and love.

But love, as they always said, is not measured by place or time, but by the people you choose to spend your time with.

And as time passed, I saw more in **Lucy** than I had seen in the past. She smiled at me differently, as if saying to me every time: You are more than just a lover, you are the one who made life revolve around me.

And we still live those moments, adding new chapters to our love. Together, we build memories, dreams, and cafés... and maybe a better world, because every moment with **Lucy** was happiness.

Love is not something you hold in your hands, nor something you put in your pocket. It is an independent being, sweeping over you suddenly as if you met yourself in a new mirror, discovering beauty you had not seen before.

It was a moment I had never felt before, feeling that today was not like any other day, but **Lucy's** day, the day of all the enchanting details I dream of and dream to see in her eyes.

Today is her birthday, and today is an unforgettable surprise. For weeks, I had been preparing for this moment in complete secrecy, without her feeling anything. I felt that this secret was what added to my longing and joy as the day drew closer.

I wanted to make her remember this moment for the rest of her life.

I had a marvelous plan, something bigger than just a simple gift, something that would make her heart leap with joy and fill her with love.

That day, I took **Lucy** by the hand to our café, the place we had built together, holding the most beautiful memories.

When she entered the café, soft, gentle music was playing, as if it had been made especially for this moment, and the lights were shimmering.

As she walked in, I greeted her with a calm smile and eyes filled with excitement. My steps guided me towards her, and I held her hands, saying, "Happy birthday to the light of my life, every year I love you more, every year you are my one and only love."

She smiled at me, unaware that what was about to happen would make her heart flutter with joy.

I took her by the hand to a certain corner of the café, where there was a small table decorated with the flowers she loved.

Then I asked her to sit down and said, "Wait here, I have something very special."

My voice carried a tone of nervousness, and she smiled with curiosity and anticipation.

I went into the kitchen for a few moments, then came out holding a wooden box in my hands, with her name engraved on the lid.

I placed the box in front of her quietly, "Open the box, my love."

Lucy cautiously opened the box and looked into it with anticipation. Inside the box, there was a golden key, accompanied by a small handwritten note. She stared at the key with questioning eyes, then read the note: "To the most beautiful woman, this key opens a world of endless love for you. Come with me, let me take you to a place that will be ours alone."

She lifted her head and looked at me, the astonishment in her eyes was clear.

"Where are we going?" she asked me, smiling shyly.

I held her hand and led her to a side door in the café.

I opened the door and guided her to another private floor that had been closed all the time, and she didn't know it existed.

When we entered, the surprise was waiting for her.

The room was adorned with warm lights, and the walls were decorated with paintings in colors she loved and flowers she favored. On one of the walls were hung pictures of us together, capturing our most beautiful moments.

In the middle of the room, there was a small table with another larger box on it.

I stood in front of her and whispered, "This place is my gift to you, a corner of our love, a small space for the world we have built and will continue to build together."

Lucy opened the other box, and inside it, there was a golden necklace encrusted with intertwined letters of our names, designed in an interlocking way with a flower, representing a part of our combined spirit.

When **Lucy** lifted the necklace in her hands, I noticed how her eyes lit up with a sudden sparkle.

She gently touched the intertwined letters of our names, as if feeling a part of me, then she lifted her head to look at me with eyes filled with astonishment and love.

In a voice full of emotion, she whispered, "**John**... this is not just a necklace; it means so much more. It's as if it carries all our love in these small letters. I will keep it close to my heart."

I couldn't help but smile as I saw her emotional reaction, then I moved closer and extended my hand, saying, "Let me put it on for you."

Lucy turned her face, and I gently held the necklace, fastening it around her neck. I noticed how beautiful she looked wearing it, as if the necklace was made to be a part of her.

After a few moments, she turned to face me again, and her smile was filled with something I had never seen before, something that made me feel every moment of my life was worth this one.

She whispered in a soft and loving voice, "You didn't just give me a necklace; you gave me a piece of your heart, **John**."

I took her into my arms, and we remained silent for a few moments, as if we didn't need words. The moment itself was enough to say everything. After that, we sat down together again, and in front of us was a small table with the birthday cake I had made for her.

I lit the candles, looked at her with eyes full of wishes, and whispered to her, "My wish for this year is to always stay by your side, to be the strength that makes you smile even on the worst days. Will you let me be that person, **Lucy**?"

She looked at me and said in a warm tone, "You don't need my permission because you are already the person I see forever by my side."

Then she leaned forward, closed her eyes to make her wish, and blew out the candles, leaving behind a warm glow that signaled all the hope we carried in this relationship.

After the celebration, we sat together in our special corner of the café, and I began to tell her about all the details I went through while preparing for this day, how I chose the necklace, how I planned the décor, and how excited I was with each step. She listened attentively, laughing from time to time, as if she saw the whole world in my eyes.

For the first time, I realized that love is creating happiness for someone else, giving every moment of your time for one of their smiles.

Chapter Seven

Don't ask me about doubt; ask me about the love that drives me to doubt.

Here is life taking us once again to a crossroads, where our love meets doubt, and questions begin to embed in the heart.

I was sitting in our café, which had become our haven, the place that witnessed our beautiful moments.

The dim light passed through the windows, but the shadows in my eyes were increasing bit by bit.

I couldn't stop thinking about that moment when **Victor** told me about things I didn't know, things I wasn't aware of.

He was talking about **Lucy** in a way I didn't like at all, about the places she visited alone, and the phone calls she hid from me.

I didn't want to believe it, but doubt began to creep into my heart little by little.

Suddenly, everything turned into chaos inside my mind. Those pieces of evidence were like ghosts haunting me, watching me from every corner. I was thinking about every word **Victor** said and every mysterious glimpse that passed before me without noticing it in time.

Could it be that **Lucy** had hidden something from me?

This thought was eating me from the inside, taking me into a maze of thinking. I knew I loved her more than anything in my life, but could it be that I was closing my eyes to something big happening right in front of me?

At that moment, **Lucy** entered the café, and the smile I used to adore was no longer the same. There was something strange in her eyes, something that told me she felt something different.

I tried to hide what was inside me, but my heart was betraying me. I saw a hint of confusion in her eyes, and I wondered if she felt something, or if I was imagining it.

She approached me, cautiously holding my hand.

"**John**, what's wrong?" she said to me in a soft voice, her eyes searching mine as if she were asking about something she didn't dare to say.

I searched her eyes, trying to find the answer I was looking for. "Nothing, just... there were some thoughts running through my mind."

The silence surrounded us for moments, as if she knew I was hiding something. But **Lucy**, as always, knew how to stay calm in times of doubt. She was looking for something inside me, as if she knew I was hiding a worry, but she refused to accuse me in her silence.

"**John**, if there's something bothering you, I'm here. Nothing matters to me more than us being together." She said these words in the tone of tenderness I was used to from her.

But inside me, the voice was screaming: **Were you really hiding everything?**

"I need some time to think," I said, trying to escape from my feelings that were driving me to doubt, even though I didn't want that to happen.

I wanted to tell her the truth, but I was afraid that the truth would destroy everything.

Days passed, and my heart was in constant conflict between trust and doubt. **Lucy** was trying as hard as she could to stay strong, as if she knew something was bothering me, but she was silent, watching me calmly as if waiting for me to be honest.

And that night, as the distance between us increased, the emotions accumulated more, entering another world. Between us, there was a bridge of hope, but doubt was trying to tear it down.

I didn't know where we were going, but I knew I needed an answer.

Days began to pass, and I found myself in a state of hesitation, torn between the hope I always saw in **Lucy's** eyes and the shadows that doubt had started to cast on that beautiful picture. **Lucy**, as always, tried her best to remain the same—kind, smiling, and full of life. But every time I saw her, my heart screamed, and I kept it inside.

Her calls, her actions, and the places she visited away from my eyes—all these details started to intertwine in my mind, troubling me, making me wonder if there was really something she had hidden from me. She had always been perfectly transparent, so what had changed now? Why was I beginning to feel distant from her world?

One morning, while we sat in the café that held all our memories, I began to watch **Lucy** in silence. She moved her hands gently as she served her coffee to me, as if she didn't notice the widening gap between us. Everything around us was the same, but I felt the air was heavy, and the smiles had become empty. I looked at her at that moment, trying to read what lay behind her eyes—those eyes I had always seen as a mirror to my soul. But today, they weren't the same. There was something in the depth of her eyes, as if she were hiding a big secret.

"**Lucy**..." I whispered her name, but the words were heavy on my tongue. I wanted to tell her what was inside me, but I was afraid of losing her.

She looked at me, as if she felt what was stirring inside me. Her eyes were filled with confusion, and her smile, despite everything, was filled with love and concern. "**John**, what's going on?"

Her heart was beating fast, and I knew she had felt the coldness between us. But I didn't want to tell the truth because I feared that truth would break something beautiful and leave a scar on our hearts we wouldn't know how to remove.

"Nothing, just some thoughts that are bothering me. I wish I could get past them, but there's a lot in my head."

She held my hand gently, as if trying to calm me. "If you need something, just tell me. I'm here for you."

I think I was searching for the words to restore the trust between us, that trust that had begun to erode bit by bit. "Is everything really okay, **Lucy**?"

She paused for a moment, then said in a calm voice, "Yes, everything is fine. But if something is bothering you, I'm here. I'm always here."

But despite her kind words, I couldn't shake off the doubt that weighed on my heart. I felt there was something missing, something absent in our relationship, but I didn't know exactly what.

I needed time, I needed to examine all these feelings and understand what was happening to me. But in the end, I was living in a closed circle of doubt and love, unable to escape it unless I opened the door I had closed with my own hands.

Lucy, despite her smile, fully understood that something was haunting me. She felt that something was different, but she chose to remain silent. She knew I wouldn't tell her everything until I was ready.

But at that moment, I wasn't ready. I needed more time to understand what was happening between us and to understand myself first. Would **Lucy** remain strong in the face of those shadows that had started to accompany us? Or would our love be subjected to another test?

Sometimes, love doesn't mean the absence of doubt. Love means holding onto each other, even in moments of doubt.

I don't want to believe what I'm thinking, but... doubts creep into my heart like smoke I can't escape from. I always thought I saw things clearly, that I could trust **Lucy** with everything, but now? Now everything has become unclear.

Today, after everything that has happened, I started doubting everything. In her eyes, in her words, in every move she makes. What if she was hiding something from me? What if the relationship I built with her, with all its love and honesty, was just an illusion in the end?

Victor had told me things I didn't know, things about **Lucy**... things she had hidden from me. Why hadn't I noticed them before? Why didn't I see the threads that were extending from beneath the surface, the threads of doubt that time was weaving?

At that moment, I felt everything starting to unravel. **Lucy** was smiling at me as she always did, but her smile bothered me more than ever. Was this smile real? Or was it just an attempt to hide something else? She was talking, but I didn't hear her words. My mind was distracted between the images **Victor** had painted for me and what I felt deep in my heart.

Then, without any prelude, I asked her the question I was afraid to ask: **Is there something between you and Victor?**

I didn't want to ask, but the words came out of me suddenly. The more I tried to suppress these thoughts, the stronger they became.

Moments of silence... then she said, surprised: **What do you mean?**

I saw the pain in her eyes, I knew I had hurt her, but how could I stop this? How could I stop doubting someone I loved with all my being? How could I be sure of something when I no longer knew the truth?

Is there something between you and **Victor?** I repeated the question.

Even though she repeatedly told me nothing happened, I couldn't believe her anymore. Was this the truth? Or was I living in a big lie?

For a moment, I was on the verge of collapsing. I didn't want to lose her, but I couldn't live with this doubt. I wanted to believe her, but at the same time, I couldn't ignore what I felt in her heart.

Then she said to me in a weak voice, but full of sadness: **John,** I love you... and I would never betray you. You are everything to me. There is nothing between me and **Victor**, I am here just for you.

Every word that came out of her was like an arrow...

I wanted to believe her, but the thoughts swirling in my mind were preventing me. How could I be the person I was before this moment? How could I be the man who loves her without doubting everything around him?

I felt like I was on the edge of a cliff. I didn't know if I would collapse and ask her to forgive me, or if I would walk away and leave everything behind.

But at that moment, when her eyes were filled with tears, I realized something...

Our love was measured not by words, but by actions. She tried to justify herself, and it was clear that she meant every word she said. But doubt obscured the truth from me.

"I love you, but doubt kills me, **Lucy**," I said as I moved away from her, trying to calm myself down.

Then I continued: Maybe we need some time. Maybe we should take a little distance to breathe... to make sure of what we are.

My heart was breaking as I said that. But in the end, what could I do? Doubt kills me. I needed space to understand myself first.

I needed time... and I didn't know if we could fix what was broken.

Chapter Eight

"Every time I see your eyes, I see everything, and every time I close my eyes, I feel like I'm losing myself. That's what I used to tell **Lucy**, but I didn't know that this path would lead us to the abyss of doubt. I didn't realize that every word, every moment of silence, and every pause between us would serve as gaps through which fear and confusion would sleep in. I watched this transformation between us, powerless to do anything.

Today was not like any other day. I woke up in the morning, just like any other day, accustomed to the routine of shared life. But there was a heavy cloud hanging in the horizon, something was different. I felt something unusual in the air, and I wanted to see her eyes, to hear her voice, that voice that always gave me hope.

But when I left my room, I didn't find her. The apartment was quieter than usual, as if it was trying to swallow me in its silence. I moved with heavy steps, searching for her in every corner, everywhere, but there was no trace of her. Her bag was still in its place, but everything else was missing, her body that used to inhabit the space...

Then my eyes fell on something on the table. It was a letter. It was written by her hand, and I held it with trembling hands.

"**John**, my love... If you are reading these words, know that I have left, but not because I don't love you. No, I love you more than ever. But I left to protect you, to preserve what remains of our love."

My heart stopped at that moment. The words were like harsh blows to my chest. My tears were falling, but I couldn't stop this inner flow of pain. The sadness was seeping into my veins in a way I couldn't imagine.

"I am not strong enough to bear this doubt. I am not strong enough to see your eyes filled with questions that I can't answer. I don't want you to doubt me, but at the same time, I don't want you to live in the hell we have become."

Everything was falling apart. How could **Lucy** be in a place far away from me? How could I live in this world without her?

"But I can't live in your doubts, **John**. I can't live in this confused mixture of love and fear. Our love used to cover everything, but it's no longer like that, everything has become complicated."

I started running around the apartment again, my eyes moving between the furniture and the things that held our memories. Those things couldn't fill the void she left, the void of her presence in my life. Why did doubt cloud our lives?

Then I remembered our last conversation. She always told me: "You have my heart, don't let this seep between us."

But I couldn't stop those thoughts that haunted me, those moments that made me doubt everything. Was it a wound from the past that I couldn't heal? Or was I just afraid of losing her?

I couldn't find an answer; the truth was fading away in that heavy silence.

"**John**, keep our love in your heart as it was, but I must go. This is better for us. Because if we continue on this path, we will lose ourselves."

Her last words hurt me; they carried an unexpected farewell. She was leaving, but she was taking everything I thought was constant in my life with her.

And what will happen now? Can I live in this world without her? My whole life had changed since the moment she entered it, and now everything became empty.

"You are a part of me, but I can no longer be part of this anxiety that surrounds us. I will not return, **John**. But I will always love you every moment."

I closed my eyes and said to myself: "We have lost something precious. But I will always love you, no matter the distance between us."

And in that moment, I began to learn that love is not just joy and comfort, but also pain and loss. I learned that love cannot always be perfect, and that sometimes, we must let go of some things to hold on to what remains of them.

Lucy's letter was the thing that shattered everything in my life, but I knew she did it because she loved me...

Not a day goes by without hearing your voice inside me, as if you're sitting here next to me, whispering words that would rearrange my scattered world...

I sit here alone, searching for your traces in the void you left behind, touching the places that used to be home to your laughter and the beat of your heart. It's as if I'm searching for you in a world that no one else inhabits, a world that has lost all its light. I know that life goes on, but it passes heavy, cold, and meaningless. The longing for you has become a part of my days...

I close my eyes and remember, I forget everything around me to relive those moments that took my breath away. Your hands in mine made me feel safe, your voice was like music that brought my soul back after I almost lost it. I wonder, how do you have the ability to leave all this behind? How could you leave without coming back? I miss you more than words can describe, and I love you in a way that no one can understand.

Sometimes, I go to the places where we used to sit together, sit in the cafes where we used to share stories, look at the seats that held our meetings, and find myself talking to your phantom, as if you are present. I tell you about my sorrows, how much I miss you, and think about the words you would say to me if you were here.

Maybe you would have told me "Stay strong," but the truth is that my strength has waned in your absence; everything has faded away with you. The people around me don't understand. How can they? None of them knew you as I did. None of them saw the light you brought into my life, the way you filled every part of my soul. You were that rare spirit, the one that cannot be repeated. And despite this separation that kills me, I can't hate you. Instead, I love you more. I feel that your absence has made you even more beautiful in my eyes, as if your love seeps deeper into my soul, settling in corners of my heart that I didn't know existed. They say separation makes love die, but your love does not die; it renews itself every time I realize how much I miss you. Sometimes, I hold my heart in my hands and talk to it as if it knows you. I say, "Do you remember how happy we were?" The answer comes without the need for words, as if the longing that resides in me becomes deeper and stronger every time I remember you. Maybe you were a lesson for me, a lesson that I have no choice but to live through, teaching me the meaning of loss. I see you in my dreams, walking toward me, smiling that smile that used to light up the darkness of my world. I reach out to you, but you disappear, like a fleeting phantom, like a breeze I cannot grasp. I open my eyes to find you are just a painful memory, just a dream that takes me back to the deepest corners of sorrow. Everything in me screams your name; longing sweeps over me every time a warm breeze reminds me of your voice, your scent, the stories you used to tell me, our conversations that stretched into the early hours of the morning. How did you become a part of my life that cannot be erased by forgetfulness? How can time pass, and you remain present in every moment, in every breath? They say time heals, but the truth is that time increases the weight of longing, as if the distance between us makes me more attached to you, as if separation makes me realize the depth of your love in my heart. I remember your last words in the letter you left, I remember how you told me you were leaving to preserve what was left of our love. How brave you were, while I am unable to take a single step away from you, unable to accept the idea that life goes on without you. Even in your departure, you acted for us, to preserve something pure within us. You were strong, and I am weak in front of your memory. Some nights, I hold my pen and write to you as if you will read my words. I write to you about me, about my broken dreams, about a love that has not died despite the distance, about a longing that accompanies me like my shadow. I write because writing is the only way I can talk to you, to share my feelings with you. Life may continue, but I live it with something missing, something that nothing else can fill. You were life, you were happiness. And no matter how many days pass, no matter how moments wither, I will remain here. I will keep waiting because I know that no matter how far you go, no matter how distant you become, you are a part of this heart, and absence cannot erase you. I will continue to live on your echoes, breathe your memories, and dream of a day that will bring us together, even if only in another life. I will keep waiting for you until my last breath, until everything ends, because simply... I have nothing but your love.

And I will stay here, in the same place where we lived our best moments. I will keep looking forward, waiting for your return, wondering how you will be when our gazes meet again. I will keep every moment, every whisper, every memory that insisted on leaving its mark within me, as if you never left. I will wait for you, not just with my heart, but with everything inside me. I will remain true to this vow, I will continue waiting for you, no matter how long it takes, no matter how much time passes, I will wait for you, because you are the beginning and the end. I will wait for you, **Lucy**, no matter how many years pass, for your return to me is not a possibility, but a certainty I await with a patience that exhausts me.

I am jealous of you... I am jealous of the moments when I am not with you, of the glances that may dwell in your eyes without my knowledge, of the thoughts that visit you and I do not know. I am jealous of the mornings that begin without me, and the nights that end with you far away from me. I am even jealous of your silence, because I fear someone else resides in it... I am jealous of the sunbeams that sneak onto your face every morning, of the raindrops that touch your hands, of everything that might make you smile while I am not by your side. I am jealous of the places you pass through and leave your fragrance in, of the memories that accompany you without me being a part of them, of everything that can dwell in your heart even for a moment. I am jealous because I want you to see everything through my eyes, for my voice to be the first thing you hear, and my features to be the last thing you glimpse. I want you to find safety only with me, for your heart to calm only between my hands. Because I want you for myself alone, for you to be my world as I am yours, for your heart to be a home no one enters but me, for me to remain the dream that never leaves, no matter how much time passes...

I miss you... as if life stopped the moment you left, as if I stopped breathing until I return to you. Every moment that passes away from you becomes heavier than the one before it, and every memory that brings me back to you increases my longing for you. I search for you in everything, in the places we used to go, in the conversations we used to drown in, in the silence that surrounded us sometimes without us noticing. I miss your conversation that used to bring me back to life, your laughter that used to fill the emptiness, and your eyes that guided me whenever I got lost in the world. Now, nothing seems the same. And despite all those days that have passed, I still miss you, as if time itself punishes me for your absence. You were my beloved, my partner in every detail of life, and today I live in a void that no one but you can fill. Your heart has left me, but I cannot escape from your memory that haunts me in every corner of this dark world I now see.

I know I wronged you, but I also know that I loved you like I never loved anyone in my life. Every moment of your absence reminds me how foolish I was to think that love would remain the same, that things would stay as they were. But the truth is, I did not realize that separation carries unbearable pain, and that love in your absence turns into a memory that sometimes becomes harsher than reality itself.

I cannot turn back time, nor can I change what happened, but I promise you that I will continue to love you despite the distances and despite the pain. I will continue to miss you even if you have left forever. Time may pass, but I know deep in my heart that no one will take your place, and that you will remain in my heart as you always were, a love that never dies. And maybe, one day, when hope returns to my life, I will find you again and tell you everything I was unable to say. But until then, I will stay here, missing you, waiting in silence, because you were, and will always be, the most beautiful thing that has ever happened in my life. How can I live in a world without you? How can I breathe while your breath was the air I lived by? I know I have made mistakes, and that life sometimes takes us to places we don't want to go, but my heart has not forgotten, and my soul is still attached to you. You were everything to me, and now, you have become the memory I live by and run from at the same time. Your face haunts me in every corner, in every moment, I feel like I am losing you again, even though I cannot distance myself from you. You may have chosen to leave, but I am still here, suffering from my longing for you, from the emptiness that cannot be filled. Maybe I was foolish for not appreciating you as I should have, but I thought that love does not change, and that we would always be together. Only today, I realized that love does not remain if we lose respect for it, if we are not willing to preserve it. And despite everything, I will not say goodbye. I cannot say it, because you are a part of my soul. Maybe I will never see you again, and maybe life will lead us in different directions, but my heart will always carry you as it did the first time. You are, as you were, still the most beautiful thing in my life, and the memory I will never be able to forget. I love you, my dear...

The End